RIVER DANGER

VISTA®
HIGHER LEARNING

Boston, Massachusetts

MATH

Sam lives in a nice house next to a river in southern Texas. Many years ago, a tall levee was built nearby to protect houses by the river when the river flooded.

Sam likes to walk along the top of the levee looking at the river below. Sometimes he and his father walk along the levee and look at the plants and animals that live near the river. Sam wants to be a biologist when he grows up. He finds the river very interesting as well as beautiful.

The weather in south Texas is usually dry, but occasionally there are sudden, heavy rainstorms. When this happens, it can **cause** the river to rise very quickly. At those times, Sam and his family have always been grateful for the big levee that protects them from the rising water.

Sam always goes down to the river after a rainstorm. There is a **gauge** on the river, so he can easily measure the exact height of a flood. After a flood, leaves and branches on the levee also mark where the flood waters were the highest.

Where, When, and Why
Rivers Flood

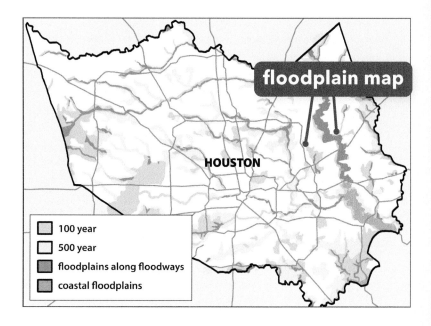

floodplain map

HOUSTON

- 100 year
- 500 year
- floodplains along floodways
- coastal floodplains

The areas along any river are divided into floodplains. These show the places that will be covered in water if the river floods. They are often divided into different regions. Certain regions are more likely to be flooded than others. Some are called two-year floodplains. They have a 50 percent chance of being flooded every year, so they flood once every two years on average. Other places are called 100-year floodplains. They have only a 1 percent chance of being flooded every year, so they flood once every 100 years on average.

Defining floodplains is very difficult. Engineers must first **estimate** how often there will be a large amount of rain. Then, they must estimate how much of that rain will go into the river.

Often the ground will take in a lot of the rain. However, buildings and streets can prevent this from happening. When it does, more water flows into rivers.

Engineers must also estimate how quickly water will flow down a river. If a river flows quickly, then the water will be carried away and the river will not rise. However, if the river does not flow quickly, the water will build up. The river may rise very high.

The elevation of a place also affects the floodplain. An area that has a low elevation is already close to water level. It's likely to flood more easily. A place that has a high elevation will only flood if the river rises very high.

This region has a low elevation. It is not much higher than the water level.

Sam keeps a **journal** that he uses to note plants and animals he sees near the river. Every time there is a flood, he also **records** the date and the height of the flood.

One day Sam was reading his journal when he saw something interesting. The floods for the year seemed to be higher than they had been the previous year. It made him wonder if the heights of the floods were increasing. He decided to ask his father about it.

The data was from the previous year. It was from the year before.

Sam told his father about how the floods seemed higher and that he thought the heights were increasing. His father listened carefully, and then he said, "You need **statistics** to **support** your **claim**. If you really want to know the answer, look at your **data set**. What's the **mean** flood height for this year?"

Sam didn't know.

"What was the highest flood this year? What was the lowest?" his father asked. "What's the **range** of flood heights for this year?"

Sam didn't know that either.

"You need to figure all of that out. It's the only way to really know if the heights of the floods are increasing," explained his father.

Sam looked at his journal and made a list of the eight floods during the year. This was his data set. He added the numbers together and came up with a **total** of 12 feet. Then he found the **average** flood height for the last year by dividing this number by 8. The mean was only 1.5 feet.

flood heights

0.89' + 1.47' + 1.08' + 0.63' + 4.5' + 1.14' + 1.53' + 0.76' = **12'**

12' ÷ 8 = **1.5 feet**

average flood height

' = feet
1.5 = one point five or one and a half

After that, Sam looked at the flood range. The lowest flood was 0.63 feet, and most of the other floods were also low. However, there was one very big flood that was 4.5 feet. "That's so much bigger than the other floods," Sam thought, "It's 3 times higher than the mean flood height. That might cause a problem. I'd better check it out!"

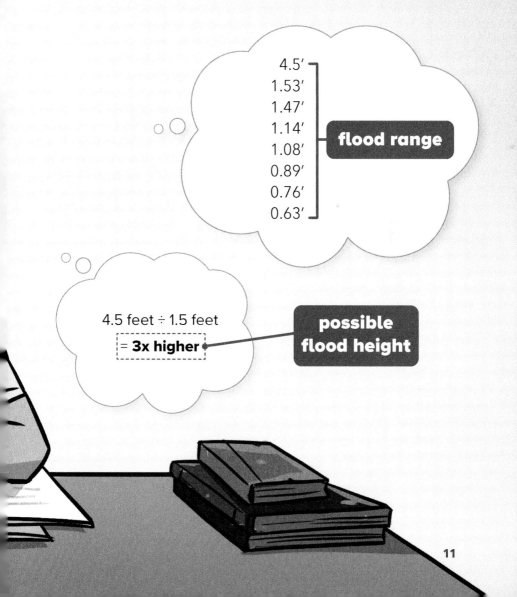

4.5'
1.53'
1.47'
1.14'
1.08'
0.89'
0.76'
0.63'

flood range

4.5 feet ÷ 1.5 feet

= **3x higher**

possible flood height

Sam looked in his journal to find data about the previous year. There had been only seven floods. This was his new data set. He did some **calculations** and found that the mean flood height for the previous year had been lower. It was only 1.3 feet. "The mean flood height this year is higher than it was last year," Sam thought. "But it shouldn't be a problem. It's still pretty low."

Sam was still worried about the floods becoming much higher than the average. He decided to talk to his father about it. "We may someday have an even bigger flood," Sam insisted to his father. "That could be dangerous!"

"Hmm, well, 4.5 feet is a big flood," admitted Father. "But the levee is 8 feet tall. A dangerous flood would have to be much bigger, so I think we're safe."

Flood Data Set Last Year

Date:	Height:
April 8	0.48 feet
May 17	1.61 feet
June 28	0.73 feet
July 4	0.81 feet
September 13	3.24 feet
October 21	1.41 feet
November 8	0.82 feet

Total Last Year

$0.48 + 1.61 + 0.73 + 0.81 + 3.24 + 1.41 + 0.82 = $ 9.10 feet

Average Flood Height Last Year

$9.10 \div 7 = $ 1.3 feet

Sam felt much better after his father said this. Then, his father said, "We'd better check to be sure. I still have my old journals where I recorded flood heights just like you do. I also have your grandmother's journals. Maybe she recorded flood heights in them, too. They could give us a bigger data set to help you support your claim. Would you like to read them?"

"Oh, yes, please!" said Sam.

14

Sam read his father's journals. He found there were fewer floods in his father's time, and that those floods were lower. Sam made a list of all the floods in his father's journals. His father had kept journals for many years, so it was a big list. Sam found that the mean flood height at that time had been only 1 foot.

Next, Sam looked in his grandmother's journals and he found flood information there, too. He made another big list and found that the average flood in his grandmother's time had been even lower—it was only 0.8 feet. "The floods *have* gotten higher!" Sam thought.

Then, Sam saw a really big flood in his grandmother's journal. It was 4.8 feet high! "Wow! That was even higher than the flood we had this year," he thought. "But the levee is 8 feet tall, so we should still be safe."

Sam thought again. "But if 4.5 feet is a big flood when the average is 1.5 feet," he thought. "Then 4.8 feet was a *huge* flood when the average was 0.8 feet. This could be really bad!"

Sam quickly went to see his father again. They might be in danger from the river!

"Dad? I did the calculations, and I'm really worried about a big flood again," Sam began. "There was a big flood in Grandmother's journal. It was six times higher than the average flood in her time. The flood average was only 0.8 feet then."

"Yes?" said his father. "Why is that important?"

"Now our average flood is 1.5 feet," explained Sam. "What if we have a flood that's 6 times higher than our average flood? Six times 1.5 feet is 9 feet! That would be higher than the levee!"

"Hmm, maybe you're right," noted his father, thinking quietly. "The journals show that the average floods are higher now. It's reasonable to think that the highest floods would also be higher. I think we'd better talk to the city about this."

Sam and his father put all of Sam's data into a report. After checking Sam's calculations, they went to see the town mayor. The mayor listened to Sam's father describe the problem. Then, Sam showed her the report with their statistics. The mayor was impressed—and a little worried!

"This data is very important," she said. "We'll have to check your numbers, but I think you have **identified** a real problem here. Well done!"

The mayor was impressed. She admired and respected Sam's work.

One year later, Sam and his father were asked to join the mayor and other town residents at a celebration on the levee. It was to mark the beginning of work on a new project. The town was building a new levee that would be high enough to protect everyone from higher floods. As part of the celebration, the mayor gave a speech.

"The river is rising and it's becoming a danger to our town," she began. "Today we begin work on a higher, stronger levee that will keep us all safe. But if one young man had not discovered this danger, we all may have suffered a terrible flood. Thank you, Sam Martinez!"

💧 River Danger Organization

River Controls

weir

Levees are the main tool engineers use to control rivers. However, there are two big problems with levees. The first problem is that levees are made of dirt. During a flood, the river can weaken the levee by carrying away the dirt. This **process** is called erosion. If it continues for too long, it will make a hole in the levee.

The worst place for erosion is at turns in the river. Engineers fight erosion at these places by building concrete reinforcements on the levee. Another way to reduce erosion is to place large blocks in the river. These are called weirs. The weirs slow down the water, so that it carries away less dirt. Erosion can also destroy a levee if it is not high enough. When water begins to flow over the top of a levee, it carries dirt off of the top of the levee.This makes the levee shorter, so more water can flow over the top. Then, even more dirt is removed from the levee, and soon there is a large hole.

The second problem with levees is a process called silting. Because of erosion, rivers carry a lot of dirt or silt. If the river slows down, then the dirt goes to the bottom of the river. Over time, this causes the bottom of the river to get higher. Then, when there is a flood, it's easier for the water to go over the top of the levee.

Engineers have several ways to fight silting. One way is to just make the levees higher. This works for a while, but the silting will continue. Then, the levee must be built even higher. (There are places on the Mississippi River where the bottom of the river is much higher than the surrounding land.)

Another way to fight silting is to place the levees close to the river. This makes the river narrow, so that the water flows quickly. When the river flows more quickly, dirt does not go to the bottom and there is less silting. Unfortunately, this fast-moving water can also make erosion worse.

A third way of controlling silting is to remove the dirt from the bottom of the river. This process requires large, expensive machines, and it takes a lot of time and effort. It also does not stop the silting, so the river must be cleaned every few years.

concrete reinforcement

cause to make something happen, often something that has a bad effect

gauge an instrument for measuring how big or how much of something there is

estimate to make an educated guess about the size, cost, or worth of something

journal a written set of notes or information kept over a longer period of time

record to write down information for use in the future

statistics a collection of numbers, measurements, and mathematical information from real-life or experimental data

support to help show that something is true or a fact

claim a statement that you believe; a piece of information you think is true even though you can't prove it and other people may not believe it

data set a collection of information, often facts or numbers, that is used to help make a decision

mean / average the result of adding a set of numbers and dividing by the number of items in the set

range the difference between the highest and lowest values in a set of numbers

total the amount found by adding two or more numbers together

calculation the process of using math to find an amount or number

identify to find a problem, fact, or need

process the actions done to get a result